Tales in Rhyme

Snow White and the Seven Dwarfs

Sia Gupta

AF516745

Om KIDZ
An imprint of Om Books International

Snow White and the Seven Dwarfs

I will tell you a tale in rhyme,
That once upon a time,
Lived a beautiful queen and her king,
They possessed almost everything.

In their life, they were missing something.
They had a vision of their baby playing.
After many-many tearful, unhappy years,
Their prayers finally reached God's ears.

They were blessed with a child
Who was wonderful and mild.
But the same day disaster struck;
The queen died, it was just bad luck!

Yet the king had a princess so sweet,
Looking at her was an absolute treat.
He named her Snow White,
For her beauty was pure and light.

Her skin was white as snow,
She was as pretty as a bow.
Her lips were red as roses,
She had no vanity, no poses.

Even though the king grieved,
He needed a wife, he believed.
He married a lady he thought was kind,
It turns out, her beauty made him blind.

The new queen was extremely vain;
The people actually thought her insane.
The king died a few months later,
And the evil queen became a dictator.

Meanwhile, the princess grew into a pretty girl,
With shiny skin and hair twisted in a curl.
She was waiting for her prince to arrive,
And was just managing to somehow, survive.

The queen had a magic mirror that spoke,
And every day when she woke,
She asked, 'Mirror, mirror on the wall,
Who is the fairest of us all?'

The mirror never, ever, lied,
It always dutifully replied,
'You are the fairest everywhere.'
Then one day it gave her a scare!

It said, ‘You are lovely, my pretty queen,
But Snow White is now, the fairest seen.’
The evil queen was furious inside out,
In her anger she was up and about.

She called her royal hunter brave,
And specific orders she gave,
‘Kill the young girl, Snow White.
If you must, use all your might!’

'For proof, I want her heart.
Understand this, Huntsman Stuart!
Bring me her bones as well,
And do exactly as I tell.'

Horrified, the hunter went to kill;
He was only doing it at the queen's will.
In the courtyard, he saw Snow White,
Dancing and singing, merry and bright.

His heart began to pound and beat;
Snow White with dignity, he wanted to treat.
She was kind to animals and humans alike,
It would be hard for him to kill or strike.

But he took out his knife all the same,
And near the princess he came.
'I must kill you princess,
For I am stuck in a mess.'

'The queen has a violent wish,
For you, from this world to vanish.'
'Please don't kill me,' with tears she said.
The hunter too did not want her dead.

He said in a loud frightening tone,
'From an animal I will get heart and bone.
You just run away, my dear.'
And Snow White fled in fear.

Without taking any comfort or rest,
Snow White ran into the wild forest.
She ran deeper into the woods,
As far and as fast as she could.

Tired, she was about to collapse;
She had never been exhausted, perhaps.
Suddenly she saw a reason to smile,
A cottage ahead, maybe she could stay a while.

'Oh, I don't think the owners would mind
If me inside their cottage, they do find.
I will make it beautiful, spick and span,'
And into the cottage she quickly ran.

With the help of a herd
Of animals as well as birds,
The house was made clean as ever.
She wished to stay there forever.

Snow White felt tired soon,
The time was almost noon.
She went upstairs falling asleep,
The owners were away in the woods, deep.

The cottage was owned by the seven dwarfs,
Some were grumpy and some full of laughs.
Everyday mining they would go,
Singing, 'Hi-ho, hi-ho hi-ho!'

That day when they came back,
The house was not dirty or black.
The cottage, they started to explore,
And found surprises, many more!

Until one said, 'Let's go up to the second floor.'
And slowly they opened the upstairs door.
Lying in their beds, sweet-smelling and clean
Was the prettiest maiden they had ever seen.

In the blink of an eye, Snow White woke
And looked at the dwarfs before she spoke.
'I'm sorry for the mess I have made,'
Snow White said, sounding quite afraid.

'Please tell me your name,
And I will tell you why I came.'
Said the dwarf, fat and tall,
'I'm Doc, the leader of us all.'

'I'm Bashful,' a shy dwarf said,
'I like to hide my body and head.'
'I'm Sneezy,' said a dwarf,
'I sneeze a lot and cough.'

'I'm Happy,' said the jolliest one,
'Full of laughter and always ready for fun.'
'I'm Sleepy,' said the dwarf with a red cap,
'I'm always ready for a quick nap.'

'I'm Grumpy and I just
Don't easily like to trust.'
'This is Dopey who cannot talk,
Though he murmurs,' said Doc.

'Now tell us why you are here,
My sweet and lovely dear.'
'I ran away,' Snow White said,
'The evil queen wants me dead.'

'I will wash and clean if I can stay,
And cook your food everyday.'
'Okay!' almost everyone cried,
Only Grumpy had not replied.

'What if the queen decides to kill us all?
We will have to flee at a moment's call!'
Said Grumpy who, like his name,
Played the 'I am Grumpy' game.

'I promise I won't cause any harm,'
Said Snow White with her innate charm.
'All right dear, you can stay,
And cook for us, you may.'

Said the dwarfs together,
'You may even stay forever!'
Then Snow White said, 'Wash your hands,
Or in trouble you will all land!'

'Yes, of course! As you say, Miss.'
Snow White in return, gave them a kiss.
'Now I will cook some nutritious food,
Which I hope will be tasty and good.'

Then the dwarfs began to eat,
Soup rice and some wheat.
As the soup, they started to slurp,
They began to grunt and burp.

Snow White wanted to snap and hiss,
'You wild hooligans, listen to this.
Now this is not what you should do,
You will have to learn manners too!'

‘You take a nice, silver spoon,
Grumpy dear, don’t you moon.
Now drink it ever so gently,
And sip quietly and lightly.’

Soon their manners improved,
And little gentlemen, they proved.
Snow White was enjoying her life,
But ahead were times of great strife.

Stuart was to kill the queen's daughter;
Snow White, he could not slaughter.
Instead, he had killed a pig,
And a false grave he did dig.

The queen was now happy and content;
She thought she had achieved her intent.
One day, she asked the mirror just for fun,
'Who is the fairest amongst everyone?'

'You are the loveliest lady, my queen,
But Snow White is the fairest, I must ween.
With seven dwarfs, she enjoys her life,
In true happiness, she still survives.'

The evil queen gave a loud cry.
She wanted Snow White to die.
The evil queen was really a witch,
An extremely rotten, nasty snitch!

She then, put poison on a pretty comb,
Preparing to go to Snow White's home.
She dressed herself to look very old,
This was a plan quite evil and cold.

She then travelled on her ride,
To the dark and dreary countryside;
Until the cottage, she finally reached,
And then loudly she screeched.

'I am a poor old woman, here to sell
A comb to you, dear, darling belle.'
'I'll take a lovely comb,' she said,
And brushed it on her shiny head.

Soon she fell and appeared dead;
The old hag cackled with glee and fled.
When the dwarfs marched through the door,
They saw Snow White lying dead on the floor.

Doc took out the comb from her hair,
While the others looked on in despair.
Suddenly, Snow White woke up again,
They jumped with joy, relieved from pain.

Meanwhile, the queen asked the mirror,
Wearing a dress that was full of glitter.
'Mirror, mirror on the wall,
Who is the fairest of us all?'

It said, 'You are the loveliest, my queen,
But Snow White is still the fairest seen.'
The angry queen made a new plan,
To cut short Snow White's lifespan.

She laced poison on to an apple,
And went to pray at the chapel.
Dressing up, she went to the countryside,
Hoping that this time, Snow White died.

Again, innocent young Snow White
Bought the fruit, taking a juicy bite.
Snow White fainted in a deadly swoon,
The queen celebrated her end as a boon.

When the seven dwarfs came back
To the cottage, unaware of the attack,
They saw their Snow White looking dead;
Next to her was lying an apple, so red.

They didn't want to bury her underground,
Wanting to see her lovely face, all year round.
So, they made her a sparkling glass coffin.
Tears flowing, choking and wailing, ever so often.

That day, a handsome prince was riding by,
He saw the commotion and wondered why.
When he saw pretty Snow White,
His eyes sparkled, blue and bright.

'Oh, please may I kiss her?
The lady makes my heart stir!'
The dwarfs looked at each other,
'Yes,' they said to him together.

As soon as the prince took a gentle dive
And kissed her, she suddenly came alive.
She woke up and turned around to see,
What luck! The spell was broken, she was free.

'Oh, my dear, darling princess!
Now I have to honestly confess,
The moment I saw you with my weary eyes,
My heart began to beat fast, my pulse did rise.'

'Will you marry me, I beg you please?
My love till the end, will never cease.'
'Of course I will,' Snow White said,
Her cheeks turned bright and red.

The prince wanted to punish the evil queen,
But kind-hearted Snow White was not keen.
The prince took charge with all his strength and wisdom,
While the wicked queen was banished from the kingdom.

The villagers were happy at the princess's return,
They even had a prince now, to look at their concern.
Everyone wanted a grand royal wedding,
It was to take place in a magnificent setting.

The happy couple couldn't stop grinning,
It was such a fantastic, grand beginning.
Snow White and the prince married in joy and laughter,
And they lived happily ever after!